HOW TO BE A HERO
FINDING THE SUPER IN YOU!

By Tracy Bryan

"A hero is someone who, in spite of weakness, doubt or not always knowing the answers, goes ahead and overcomes anyway."

Christopher Reeve (Superman)

Author/Publisher Disclaimer

The information contained in this book is provided as an information resource only and is not to be used or relied on for any diagnostic or treatment purposes. Please consult a certified Child Health Care Professional before making any health care decisions that are discussed in this book. The author and publishers expressly disclaim responsibility and shall have no liability for any loss, damages or injury whatsoever suffered as a result of a person's reliance on the information contained in this book. The information in this book is opinion of the author and has also been researched and cited as necessary.

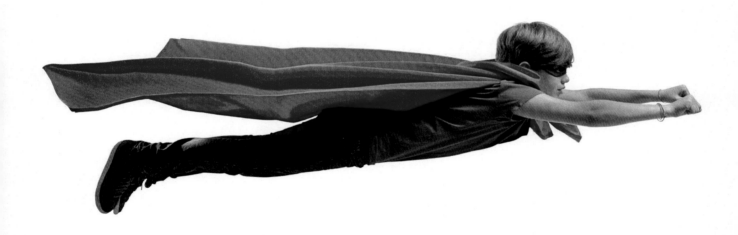

HOW TO BE A HERO
FINDING THE SUPER IN YOU!

By Tracy Bryan

What is a Hero?

In the comics, movies and on TV, there are SUPER HEROES. These larger than life people have powers to battle their enemies, fight for justice and save the day!

These super humans have the ability to fly, are able to leap tall buildings, swing through the cities on webs and run across the world. They can possess great speed and get from one place to the next really fast. Superheroes have amazing strength that allows them to lift, move and throw just about anything. They have the capacity to go the distance with any task because their strength and will enables them to do this. Some superheroes can read minds because they have the power of telepathy, while other ones have super sight and can see with x-ray or infrared vision. Some of them even have invisibility and they can go somewhere and hide out or sneak up on their enemies. The best quality of all these superheroes is probably the healing ability-they can recover quickly from injury, never have illness and heal other people!

These are all really cool qualities and abilities to have, but unfortunately there are no real humans like this. There are real life, EVERYDAY HEROES though...

There are so many everyday heroes out there in the world and if you look hard enough you can see them. These people are women, men and children that use their human qualities and abilities to LEARN, LOVE, SHARE, TEACH and RISK in order to help other people. These super people use education, compassion, connecting, inspiration and sacrifice to spread their hero-ness through the world and make it a better place for everyone.

These are regular people who take their natural abilities that we're all born with and use them for good. They do this because they care about themselves and everyone around them. Everyone is capable of being an everyday hero...
YOU CAN BE A HERO TOO!

"You're much stronger than you think you are. Trust Me"
Superman

How can YOU be an everyday hero? Everyone can be a hero with the abilities to learn, love, share, teach and risk...

LEARNING-education is very important in being a hero because the ability to LEARN is a gift-the more we know about something, the more we can understand it. When we understand how things work, why they work a certain way and what we can do with them, it's so much easier to function in our world. If we understand how to function, this helps us solve problems and figure out solutions for everyday challenges.
Learning gives us basic abilities and skills that we can use everyday-walking, eating, writing, talking, etc. If we didn't learn how to do these when we were babies, we wouldn't be doing them now. As we get older and as we grow, we learn new things everyday to help us function throughout our life.

Usually we learn new abilities as we need them-we didn't learn how to write when we were babies because we couldn't even hold a pencil. We learn in different stages of growth.

In each stage of human growth, we learn more and more skills to get us to the next stage. Learning can go on throughout a person's life. Some people may stop learning at certain points in their life because they get stuck at different stages of growth. These are usually the grumpy people of the world who are miserable though, and they forget to look for all the wonderful things about their life!

One of the most important parts about being an educated hero is learning about other people. Heroes should have an interest in UNDERSTANDING people. People are interesting! They have so many feelings, thoughts and needs. Learning about other people means listening and being open to hear what other people have to say. When we listen to other people's feelings and needs, we learn so much about them and our understanding of them helps them too.

"Why do we fall? So we can learn to pick ourselves up"
Batman

LOVING- is very important in being a hero because the ability to love means that we know how to have affection for someone else.

Being able to LOVE is so great because when we love someone they almost become a part of us, we attach meaning to it-to them. We love our family because it's ours and we care about it. Having meaning for things in life gives us a chance to connect with other people, which gives us purpose for being on this earth and reasons to keep living here.

We can love in so many different ways-love for our family is different than how we love our friends. The nice thing about having love for other people is that they love us back. It's amazing how easy it is to love people- you would think that it must take a lot of energy to love all the people that we love in our life. Actually, it hardly takes any energy because it gives us energy and good feelings to love people.

A big part of loving people is having COMPASSION for them. Compassion is when we feel so much love that it also gives us the ability to feel how other people are feeling too. We can 'put ourselves in someone else's shoes' and imagine what they are feeling. Having compassion means putting other people's needs before our own and thinking about what we can do to bring them happiness.

We have compassion for someone we love when we try to make them smile or laugh. This brings happiness to them and it's important to make the people we love feel good. We have compassion when someone we love is upset or facing something difficult in their life by wishing we could help them and trying to make them feel better.

Everyday heroes will stop at nothing to defend the people they love. Having compassion also means protecting the people we love because we want them to be safe.

"Sometimes to do what's right, we have to give up the things we want the most"
Spiderman

SHARING- is very important in being a hero because the ability to SHARE brings such pleasure to other people and makes them feel included. This is especially true when we share our ideas and feelings with other people. Heroes may seem like they work alone, but with the help and support of other people, heroes can accomplish so much more.

Heroes inspire other people to do the right thing. Sometimes there are group situations in life where a decision needs to be made or an action started- a leader is needed. The leader is the hero in this situation because they encourage other people to decide fairly or they guide others how to act.

It's difficult being the leader of both of these situations and it takes a lot of courage to share our ideas with everyone else. What if other people don't like our ideas and they laugh or tease us? A hero that leads must always feel like their ideas will benefit and be fair to everyone involved no matter how people react to them. When they believe this to be true, heroes also know that sharing was well worth the effort.

Sometimes heroes need to share their FEELINGS too. Keeping everything inside and not expressing our feelings is far too harmful to any person. People who don't talk about their feelings usually become really unhappy in their life and they get kind of grumpy.

It's difficult to talk about our feelings sometimes though. We need to find someone that we can really trust to share these with. Everybody needs to have someone like this in their life because it can feel really lonely when we keep our feelings buried deep inside ourselves and don't get them out of our body.

Usually, most problems and awful feelings can be talked or worked out. If we don't work them out, it can feel like we have the weight of the world on our shoulders!

"When you decide not to be afraid, you can find friends in super unexpected places"
Ms Marvel

TEACHING-is very important in being a hero because the ability to TEACH helps the people that need to learn.

We already know that the reason we need to learn is to gain the basic abilities and skills that we can use everyday. We need someone to teach us these though, so learning doesn't happen unless teaching is involved. Teachers are essential in the learning process. The people that teachers are teaching will eventually be the new teachers and leaders, once they have learned everything that they need to know.

We first learn how to function from our parents-we learn our basic skills and needs that keep us healthy, happy and out of danger. When we are ready to go out into the world, the school teachers take over. School teachers help us learn our social and educational needs. Throughout our life, we have many teachers and places of learning- family, friends, people at school, afterschool activities, clubs and then work. Even strangers teach us certain rules of what to say and how to act in social situations.

There is no specific age to be a teaching hero. Some teachers start teaching really young. As long as there is someone that needs to learn something, a teacher is needed.
So, every teaching hero was once taught by a teacher too!

Heroes get their wisdom and their inspiration from their teacher. INSPIRATION is like a tickling of the mind that gives someone a good feeling.

When the hero is inspired, it's their job to inspire someone else. Our parents inspire us to be good people when they tell us how proud they are of us or give us hugs because they want to spread their love to us. School teachers, babysitters, grandparents and many other people in our life inspire us everyday, which helps us to become inspiring heroes. Life is pretty tough though, so knowing we have people behind us is great to know. During really challenging times, remembering the love and inspiration of these people helps us get through even the most difficult of situations!

"Life doesn't give us purpose, we give life purpose"
The Flash

RISKING–is very important in being a hero because the ability to RISK means doing whatever it takes for what we believe in.

Risking something for what we believe in is also called making a sacrifice. A sacrifice is a choice that we make to lose or give something up. Choosing to give something up is really difficult, especially when that thing we are giving up has value to us. Just like when we share a piece of our candy with a friend or lend them our favorite video game, we are giving up and sacrificing this valuable thing for the good of our friendship.

A hero makes sacrifices like this all the time. They have a goal of saving the world, so they may have to sacrifice other things in their life that are valuable to them. Usually, all superheroes have to sacrifice their family life–most can't get married or have kids because they are too busy saving the world. It's too dangerous for a super hero to have a family, because with every superhero there is also a villain!

All heroes are determined to reach their goals no matter what they must SACRIFICE. The way they see it is that they believe in their goals so much, and they have such value in these goals, that sacrifice is worth it, if the goals benefit others. They will stop at nothing to accomplish these goals because they are so determined.

Everyday heroes can be determined too. If there is something that we really believe in (like a friendship) we will do whatever it takes and sacrifice for this important thing. Sacrificing doesn't have to be something huge, it can be a little thing- like thinking about someone else before ourselves or giving something away to someone that needs it. A very simple way to sacrifice is standing up for someone who is being bullied. Even if it means getting teased ourselves, it's worth using our words to defend someone who is in need of help.

"I have no idea where I'm going to be tomorrow, but I accept the fact that tomorrow will come and I'm going to rise to meet it"
Wonder Girl

Just because we can't fly, doesn't mean that we can't LEARN to be a pilot and then fly someday. There are many pilots that fly around the world and do good deeds. Some pilots put out fires, carry sick kids to hospitals, rescue people and some fly to help the whole country in the air force.

Just because we can't read minds with the power of telepathy, doesn't mean that we can't put ourselves in someone else's shoes and feel compassion for them. It feels wonderful to LOVE someone and then put their needs before our own sometimes. Also it makes them feel great.

Just because we can't heal other people, doesn't mean that we can't bring happiness to others and SHARE our ideas, dreams and feelings with them. Who needs the ability to heal when we can make changes in other people's lives everyday, just by sharing a little bit of ourselves with them and letting them know how much we love them.

Just because we can't make ourselves invisible, doesn't mean that we can't silently TEACH and inspire people that need it. Without them even knowing, we can teach others all the important ways to be a hero-like giving someone a hug and showing them that we care, and we don't even have to say a word!

Just because we can't possess great speed or have amazing strength, doesn't mean that we can't have the ability to risk for something that we believe in. We can go the distance with any task because this kind of strength and will also comes from sacrifice. Everyday heroes can sacrifice too, especially when it means it will benefit other people. If there is something that we really believe in (like a friendship) everyday heroes will RISK and sacrifice for this!

Everyday heroes are SUPER

and ANYONE can be an everyday hero...

...even YOU!

How To Make Superhero Costumes

Rocket Fueled Jet Pack- Link doodlecraftblog.com
Sure the Rocketeer wasn't much of a superhero, but armed with a jetback and some serious do-gooder skills, any kid is bound to have a super time. Using cardboard, webbing, spray-painted two-liter bottles and some felt, they'll be thanking you for a job well done before you can say 'blast off.'

Towel Superhero Capes- Link lizardnladybug.blogspot.com
How does a superhero dry off after a swim? With a terry cloth cape, of course. Grab a towel in your preferred color, some velcro for the closure, a letter stencil, and some fabric paint to jumpstart a few (post)aqua man adventures.

No Sew Superhero Mask
No sew, no problem. Get your superhero up and running in no time with a little felt, ribbon, scissors, and five minutes. Incredible speed, indeed.

Superhero Costumes with Accessories- Link marthastewart.com
Some superheroes need a sidekick, but other just need some really rad accessories. These projects presented by Martha Stewart pay close attention to all of the important details that aid in their quest for truth and justice.

Initial Applique Cape- Link sewlikemymom.com
A sleek satin cape outfitted with your initial will definitely result in some super human strength...or just a ton of confidence. This detailed tutorial makes the felt applique process almost as easy as throwing it on and shouting "Up up and away!"

No Sew Cuffs- Link seekatesew.com
Sometimes duking it out with your arch nemesis requires nothing more than your powers and some awesome wrist cuffs. Felt, velcro, and cool printable shapes are all you'll need to piece together these must-have accessories.

Adapted from kidcrave.com

Superhero Activities & Games

Super Hero Bean Bag Attack

Each little superhero takes their turn trying to knock the villains down with bean bag attackers. You can use empty 2-liters or soda cans to create the targets. Paint the bottles or cans bright colors then just print out picture of villains and glue them to the front. Voila... your targets are ready.

For bean bags you can make them our small socks filled with dry beans or rice. Simple fill sock half way with beans, tie closed with a rubber band, then fold the sock back over itself.

Alternative: If it's a warm enough day and the party is outdoors you can use water pistols instead of bean bags. For this I would make sure to use cans as targets.

Kryptonite Disposer Race

Kryptonite is poison to superhero powers. In this superhero game the little superheroes break into two teams and race to remove all the pieces of kryptonite without touching them with their hands. To make kryptonite, ball up aluminum foil and paint them green.

To Play: Divide guests into two teams and have them form a line. Provide each team with two dowel sticks and enough kryptonite balls for every player, maybe two for every player. On the other end of the party space place two baskets (buckets, boxes, laundry baskets will all work) On the start of go one member from each team use their krypto sticks(dowel stick) to grip the kryptonite balls and run them over to their teams bucket. They run back and pass the krypto sticks to the next player. The race continues until one team gets all their kryptonite into the basket.

For younger children: you can play a non competitive version of these games where they all work as one team to remove the kryptonite. You can also use large plastic shovels instead of sticks for them to pick the kryptonite up with.

X-Ray Vision

The superheroes practice their x-ray vision skills by reaching into mystery bags and trying to guess what the objects are by touch only. This superhero game is as simple as filling some brown paper lunch bags with different household objects or even food such as popcorn, an apple cut in half, broccoli florets. Use your imagination and you'll come up with all kinds of things.

Joker's Stone Face Challenge

This is one of the superhero party games that require no props. The little superheroes are in training to be prepared for the bad guys underhanded tricks. In this game the superheroes are stuck in one of the Joker's villainous traps and the only way to escape is to make it through without laughing.

Each guest gets a chance to be Joker and has one minute to do their best to make the other players laugh. They earn a point for everyone who laughs.

Catch the Villian

The little superheroes must chase the villain and try to catch him with their lightening ring (hula hoop). When one lassoes the villain he throws out candy for his release. The game continues until all the candy is gone.

To play you'll need a fun spirited adult to play the part of the villain. You'll also need a bag full of candy and a hula hoop for each child. You can often find hula hoops at the dollar store for a buck. If you are on a tight budget you can eliminate the hula hoops and just have superheroes tag the villain. You'll want to play this game in a large space. A yard will be perfect.

Super-Duper Obstacle Course

The little superheroes practice their superhero skills with a super-duper obstacle course games. The course can be created from all kinds of household objects. You can even mix in mini-games through out the course.Some fun ideas for obstacles are can be:

Running through hula hoops

Jumping on a pile of cushions or pillows.

Have them limbo.

Shoot a rocket through a hoop or a target. (find cheap rocket guns at the dollar store)

Pop a balloon

Karate chop a bad guy (you can use a cushion or bop bag for the villain)

Climb through a tunnel.

Weave in and out of cones (cones can be anything)

Bust through a wall. Stack up cardboard boxes to make wall.-   Spin around on a bat.

Let your imagination run wild and set the course up however you want with whatever you've got. You can play for best time or just let them run through the games and obstacles for fun. Award prizes for all kids when they've reached the finish.

Phone Booth Dress-Up Relay

It is important as a superhero to conceal your true identity. In this superhero party game the guest race to put on an oversized blazer, shoes and glasses and run to their teams phone booth to change out of the disguise and into the superhero cape, mask and boots. They then rush back to their team and remove the superhero costume and pass it to the next member of their team. The first team whose members complete the race wins!

You can make a phone booth out of an empty refrigerator box. You can find these at appliance stores for free. Next you'll need to find the costume props. You can find these at a thrift store if you don't have them already. Make a cape using an old pillow case. Masks can be bought at the dollar store.

Find the Villian

Print out individual pictures from the net of all the superheroes you can think of and their villains. Next, tape or glue the pictures onto index cards. Examples: Spiderman - Sandman, Green Goblin, doctor Octopus
Batman- Joker, Penguin, Mr. Freeze
Superman - General Zod, Lex Luther, Ultraman
Hint: if you Google the superheroes name with the word enemies you'll find all the info you need. Search Google images for pictures. First hide the villain cards all around the playing area. Then have each player draw a superhero card. They must find the enemies of that superhero. You can provide names and pictures of the villains they are looking for to make it easier.

Spidey-Sense Obstacle Course

Each person gets a turn to make their way through the obstacle course and collect Spiderman's spiders without knocking over any cones. The trick is they have to do it blind folded with only their fellow superhero trainees guiding them through with their voices. To play this game you'll need to set up some barriers (cones, cushions, boxes) in the play zone. You'll also need to purchase some toy spiders and spread them through the play zone also. Blind fold one player at a time, making sure they cannot peek. The other players can use their voices to guide the person around the barriers and obstacle to find the spiders. You can play without keeping score or you can give each player 1-2 minutes to collect as many spiders as they can without knocking over any barriers.

Mission Blast

While the music is playing the little superheroes must try to keep all the balloons, or mission blast, up in the air. When the music stops they all grab one. A players name is drawn from a bag and that player must then pop their balloon and complete the challenge inside (XXXX) to win a small prize. The music starts again and the game continues until every guest has won a prize. To make mission blast simply write out simple challenges on slips of paper and insert them into balloons before blowing them up. Challenges should be simple and fun, some examples are:
Rub your stomach while patting your head.
Stuff two marshmallows in your mouth and sing the happy birthday.
Crabwalk across the floor.
Sing your favorite song in a funny voice
Try and lick your elbow
Say the alphabet backwards
To play you'll need twice as many balloons as guests. Start the game with one balloon for each guest and add one after each round. This is to ensure that the person whose name is called always has a balloon. This is a great non competitive game where everyone gets to participate.

Adapted from queen-of-theme-party-games.com

A Message From The Author...

I loved watching cartoons on the weekends. I would wake up early on Saturday mornings, go to the family room, make a fort with my pillows and sheets, grab my cereal and hang out all morning watching cartoons. Eventually, my mom would send me outside to get some fresh air, but that didn't stop me. There, I would continue my fun by imagining that I was Super Girl saving the neighborhood. I loved those early mornings watching and being my favorite super hero- it was magical! I was pretty young then, but I still get that feeling when I want to help someone or do a good deed for someone else. It feels great helping others and its amazing how much we CAN make the world a better place- just by using our everyday human abilities of LEARN, LOVE, SHARE, TEACH and RISK! Now... go save the world! Trace:)

Do you have all the
abilities it takes to be
a HERO?

Everyday Heroes make a difference in the world by using their
special abilities! Discover what these abilities are and find out
how you can be an everyday hero...find the SUPER in you!